THERE WAS AN OLD LADY WHO SWALLOWED THE A B C s

With special thanks to:
Cool & Capable Copyeditor Catherine Weening,
Dynamite Designer Dave Neuhaus
& Marvelous Master of Meter Marie O'Sullivan.

Text copyright © 2020 by Lucille Colandro
Illustrations copyright © 2020 by Jared D. Lee Studios

ISBN 978-1-338-65623-7

10 9 8   21 22 23 24

Printed in the U.S.A.   40
First printing 2020

Book design by David Neuhaus

THERE WAS AN OLD LADY WHO SWALLOWED THE A B C s

By Lucille Colandro

Illustrations by Jared Lee

Scholastic Inc.

There was an old lady who swallowed 26 letters.
She ate them too fast – she should have known better!

Back out they tumbled, from A down to Z.
So let's follow along and learn the ABCs.

apple pie

alligator

astronaut

ant

A is for **alligator**, **astronaut**, and **apple pie**.

Bb

birds

butterfly

bumblebee

bugs

B is for **birds**, **bugs**, and **butterfly**.

C is for cactus, car,
and a chicken that clucks.

Dd

ducks

daisy

dog

D is for a **dog digging daisies**
and two **dancing ducks**.

E is for **Earth**, **eggs**,
and an **elf** in disguise.

Ff

fish

frog

flowers

flies

F is for **fish**, **flowers**,
and a **frog** catching **flies**.

G is for **gold**, **green goblins**, and **ghosts** out at night.

H is for a **horse** at a **hoedown** —
oh, what a sight!

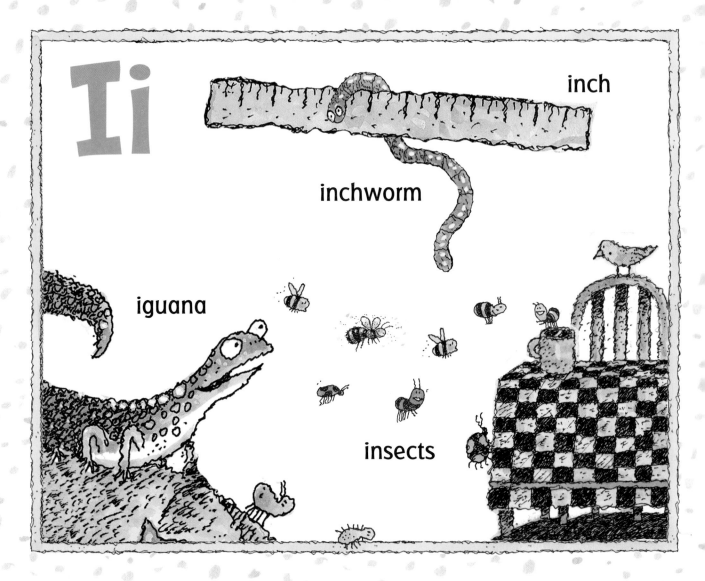

Ii

inch

inchworm

iguana

insects

I is for inchworm, an iguana,
and insects invited to tea.

jet

jewel

jalopy

Jeep

J is for **jet**, **Jeep**, **jewel**,
and an old **jalopy**.

Kk

kite

kazoo

kitten

key

K is for **key**, **kite**,
and a **kitten** playing **kazoo**.

Ll

luck

love

lizard

little thing

L is for sending **love**, **luck**,
and **laughter** to you.

Mm

man in the moon

mermaid

magician

M is for mermaid, magician, and man in the moon.

N is for number nine
and the planet Neptune.

Oo

ocean

octopus

oyster

O is for **oyster**, **octopus**,
and **other** things in the **ocean**.

Pp

parrot

presents

pup

P is for **party**, **presents**, and **pets** causing commotion.

queen

quarterback

Q is for **quick**, **quarterback**, and **queen**.

rainbow

rose

rabbits

rocks

R is for **rabbits**, **rose**, and the most **radiant rainbow** you've ever seen!

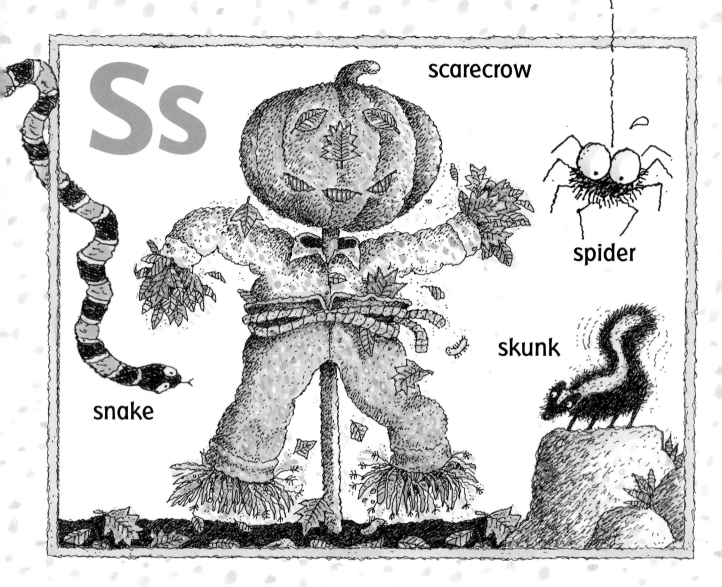

Ss

snake

scarecrow

spider

skunk

S is for scarecrow, spider, and more spooky stuff.

Tt

turtle

truck

tugboat

tractor

T is for **tugboat** and **turtle**
and **things that** are **tough**.

U is for **umbrellas** and
ukuleles **up** in space.

Vv

valentine

HAPPY VALENTINE'S DAY! Love, The Old Lady

violin

vase

V is for **violin**, **valentine**,
and a rose in a **vase**.

W is for **wind**, **wave**, **water**, and **whale**.

X marks the spot

X marks the spot
in a pirate's tale!

Yy

yellow

yawn

Y is for **yawn**,
and a bright **yellow** sun.

Zzzz is for sleep when the **ABC**s
are all done.

Hooray! The old lady is happy to see
that you now know your ABCs!